Brew
Books X7

BREWITT

Clown

QUENTIN BLAKE

HENRY HOLT AND COMPANY

NEW YORK

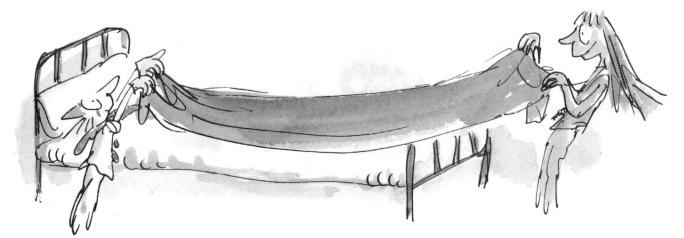

Henry Holt and Company, Inc.
Publishers since 1866
115 West 18th Street
New York, New York 10011

Henry Holt is a registered
trademark of Henry Holt and Company, Inc.

First published in the United States in 1996 by Henry Holt and Company, Inc.
Originally published in Great Britain in 1995 by Jonathan Cape,
a division of Random House UK Limited.
Library of Congress Cataloging-in-Publication Data
Blake, Quentin. Clown / Blake.
Summary: After being discarded, Clown makes his way
through town having a series of adventures as he tries
to find a home for himself and his other toy friends.
[1. Toys—Fiction.   2. Home—Fiction.   3. Stories without words.]   I. Title.
PZ7.B56C1   1996   [E]—dc20   95-12811

ISBN 0-8050-4399-3

First American Edition—1996
Printed in Hong Kong
1   3   5   7   9   10   8   6   4   2
The artist used watercolor and ink to create
the illustrations for this book.